Goodnight Two Minute Tales

Brown Watson
ENGLAND

© 2014 Brown Watson, England
Printed in Malaysia

Freddy Fire Engine

Freddy is a handsome, shiny fire engine who loves his job. Usually, Freddy is very busy putting out house-fires and rescuing people and animals from blazing buildings or tall trees. But this morning Freddy is bored because there is nothing to do. He stares out of the fire station window at the cold, wet streets and decides to motor around the village to see if any of his friends are about.

But the streets are empty and the cars are tucked away in their cosy, warm garages. The only sign of life is a group of school children and their parents gathered by the side of the river. The heavy rain over the past few days has swollen the river so much that in places it has burst its banks. The only way to get the children to school is to cross the river using the little bridge.

Although the river is calm today, the bridge is still partially submerged and no one wants to wade through the muddy waters. Freddy feels sorry for the children and wants to help them. He lowers his ladder to the ground so that two little boys and their daddy can climb onto the rungs. They sit down, holding on tightly and very slowly Freddy extends the ladder all the way across the river to the path on the other side.

Then he retracts the ladder and takes the next family safely over. Half an hour later, everybody is safely on their way to school. At four o' clock, Freddy is back at the riverbank to transport everyone safely across once more. Freddy has saved the day and he's really enjoyed himself. It always feels nice to do a good turn. Freddy drives back to the fire station with a broad smile on his face.

Lazy Afternoon

One hot day in sunny South Africa, a fat bee buzzes around a little lion cub called Amber, as she dozes in the long grass. Amber flicks her tail to shoo it away but it just won't leave. Amber opens one eye and debates whether it's worth chasing the annoying bee. Then the bee lands on Amber's nose to clean itself. Amber swats the insect with her paw and scratches her nose. She leaps up and tries to catch the bee but it's too quick for her and she ends up chasing the silly insect all around the other sleeping lions.

When she barges into her dad, a huge brown lion with a magnificent mane, he leaps to his feet and roars so loudly that Amber's ears ring! Then she clambers over her sleeping mum, races around the tree and finally collapses, exhausted, on top of her brother and sister. Dad is always very grumpy if he's woken up and Mum is annoyed that Amber has disturbed the two younger cubs. Amber is ordered to lie down by the acasia tree and not move until supper time. The bee zigzags across the grass and laughs at Amber as she flops down in the shade, sighing noisily.

4

The annoying bee is gaily doing somersaults over Amber's head and buzzing so loudly that Amber knows she won't be able to fall asleep. Then Amber hears another buzzing noise and sees an enormous queen bee homing in on the smaller one. The little bee was supposed to be collecting pollen to make honey for the queen, instead of teasing the little cub. Amber watches in amusement as the two bees make lots of angry noises and bang into each other. Then the queen bee escorts the naughty little bee back to the hive. Amber snuggles down in the dry grass with a smile on her face and thinks, maybe it's not such a bad day after all.

Roger Rocket's Maiden Voyage

Roger Rocket is training to be a qualified space rocket and today is his first flight into space. He takes a deep breath and begins the countdown: '5,4,3,2,1 - we have lift off!' Roger's engine explodes into life and he streaks up into the clouds. He heads towards the Moon, marvelling at the shining stars all around him. He orbits the Moon twice before Command Centre order him back to Earth. The first flight is a success and Roger is already planning the next one, it may be to Mars or perhaps even further away. Roger can't wait!

Foolish Flower Fairy

There are hundreds of flower fairies living in the woods near you! They are almost impossible to see because they disguise themselves so well. Fairy Bluebell has long blue hair, a pretty dress made from bluebell petals and a bluebell hat. You will never see her when she stands still amongst her flowers because she blends in so well. Fairy Clover is almost invisible too when she stands in her flowers with her clover hat and dress and her pretty pink hair.

However you might spot Fairy Buttercup. She hates the colour yellow so she has dyed her yellow hair purple, her yellow dress red and her yellow hat black! But she still loves the smell of buttercups so that is where she spends her time. One day a little girl skips into the wood to pick a posy of flowers for her granny and immediately sees Fairy Buttercup. She tries to catch her, but the fairy flutters away just in time.

The little girl chases Fairy Buttercup all the way through the wood. The tiny fairy is exhausted, so she throws herself into a muddy puddle then curls up next to a pile of stones. It's a perfect disguise. The little girl hunts amongst the leaves and pebbles for a while and gives up and goes back into the wood to collect her flowers. Fairy Buttercup finds a clean stream to wash out her hair colour. Then she finds a clump of buttercups to make into new yellow clothes. She decides she much prefers yellow after all!

High in the Sky

Robert is flying to Spain today. He's feeling nervous because he has never been on an aeroplane before. Daddy hauls the suitcases onto the conveyer belt and they disappear through a gap in the wall. They seem to be waiting for ages before it's their turn to board the plane and Robert squirms with excitement. They climb the steps up to the aeroplane. It's enormous! How can this thing fly?

7

The air hostess sees that Robert is worried and offers to take him to meet the pilot after take-off. Robert can't believe his luck. The plane taxies down the runway, then speeds up to leave the ground. Robert watches the buildings getting further and further away. The houses are almost too small to be seen. Then suddenly they are over the sea. It seems to stretch forever! The air hostess comes back and takes him to the cockpit. The captain is very friendly and lets Robert sit in the co-pilot's chair.

The captain has a break while the automatic pilot flies the aeroplane. He tells Robert about the different countries he has flown to and Robert is enthralled. The captain shows Robert how he uses the panel of instruments to fly the plane. Robert asks if he can be a pilot when he grows up. The captain says if he works hard at school and does well in his exams then he might well become a pilot. Robert has a wonderful holiday in Spain but the most enjoyable thing for him was definitely the flight.

Woodland Clean-up

There is a wood near Dominic's house that used to be really pretty but is now full of litter. The woodland path is lined with empty cans, cigarette ends, sweet wrappers and plastic bags. Dominic never drops litter anywhere other than in a bin and he wishes everyone else would do the same. Dominic's mum suggests he forms a clean-up group with his classmates to tidy the wood. Dominic's teacher likes the idea and arranges a day in the wood for the class. Everyone is issued with rubber gloves and a large bin liner.

The class work their way through the trees picking up rubbish as they go. Dominic's teacher keeps a close eye on her pupils and tells them what to remove and what to leave. At the end of the day they have thirty bags full of litter and a very tidy wood. When the local newspaper hears about their efforts, they take photos of the wood and the children and write a wonderful article about the clean-up. The Mayor presents the school with an award for caring about the environment and the local council provide two litter bins for the wood. Dominic is very happy now because the wood is litter free and pretty once again. Clever Dominic!

Fish in a Fix

In the warm, sun-drenched waters of the Caribbean Sea is a beautiful coral reef. It looks like an underwater garden, but instead of flowers it is covered in pretty anemones, starfish, plants and sponges. Lots of exotic fish live amongst the coral, like Peter Puffer Fish who is playing hide and seek with Lily Lobster, Suki Squid and Pippa Pipefish. Suddenly, a huge shadow slides over the coral blocking out the sunlight.

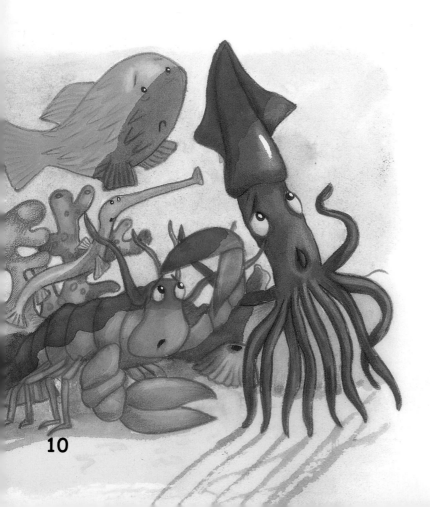

Panic hits the reef and shoals of fish dive for cover as Grumpy the Shark glides lazily towards them. Grumpy casts a hungry eye over the darting fish then turns his attention to Peter and his friends, who seem too terrified to move. Suddenly, Grumpy lunges at them and they all rush to hide in the reef. Lily and Suki find holes at the bottom of the coral, Pippa, being long and thin, squeezes into a narrow crevice and Peter squashes into another cavity.

But when puffer fish are afraid, they stick out their spikes and puff themselves up to become twice their normal size. Peter is now so big that he's jammed in tight and cannot move. Grumpy circles their hiding places trying to find a way to catch the fish. Each time he gets too close to Lily Lobster she nips his nose with her powerful pincers. Each time he gets too close to Suki Squid she squirts clouds of ink at him.

He thinks Pippa Pipefish is far too small to be worth eating, so he turns to Peter. But there is no way Grumpy can prize Peter out of his hole. Eventually he gives up and swims away. Peter calls for help. Lily and Suki don't know how to rescue him but Pippa Pipefish comes to his aid. Her long thin body fits easily into the hole. She gives Peter a big push and out he pops. They swim away from Grumpy's territory and have fun playing hide and seek until it's bedtime.

Dippy Diplodocus

Dippy Diplodocus is a very sensible dinosaur. His two best friends, Stiggy Stegosaurus and Tilly Triceratops, are always finding themselves in trouble and teasing Dippy for not joining in. Today they are having a picnic at the edge of the forest. They are not allowed to go inside the forest because scary dinosaurs like Tyrannosaurus Rex live there. When Tilly kicks the ball into the trees she and Stiggy race into the forest to find it.

Dippy calls them back but they pay no attention and soon find themselves deep in the forest. The massive trees tower far above their heads, blotting out most of the sky and they realise the ball is well and truly lost. And so are they! Just ahead, the trees appear to thin out so Stiggy and Tilly squeeze between the massive trunks and burst into a clearing. They flop down on a pile of rocks and hope someone comes to find them soon.

As they wait, they hear the sound of heavy footsteps in the distance. They are coming closer and closer every second and the ground shakes with the force of them! There is only one beast capable of so much noise. It's the terrifying Tyrannosaurus Rex! Stiggy and Tilly dive under the rocks just as T. Rex strides over their hiding place. 'Oh why won't someone rescue us?' sobs Tilly.

At the edge of the forest, Dippy watches as T. Rex thunders through the trees. He waits until he's long gone then shouts loudly for his friends. Stiggy and Tilly's mums hear Dippy calling and come to help, but the trees are too thick to see through. Then Dippy has an idea, he stands the two mums together and climbs onto their backs. Dippy has such a long neck that he can see over the top of the trees and his friends can see him. He guides them back to safety and they get a strict telling off. Clever Dippy, I don't think they'll tease him anymore!

Sleep Over Party

Tonight Hannah is having a 'sleep over' party with her three best friends: Michelle, Rosie and Alice. The three girls arrive at Hannah's home at five o'clock and rush upstairs to lock themselves in Hannah's bedroom. They have a list of 'THINGS TO DO'. First they wash their hair and pin it up in Hannah's mum's pink rollers.

While their hair is drying, they experiment with the odd bits of make-up that Rosie's mum has donated to the 'sleep over'. The lipstick proves to be particularly difficult! The girls have all brought their favourite party clothes and every bit of jewellery they can find. These all go on next. Soon it's time to take the rollers out. 'WOW!' gasps Hannah as she unravels Alice's hair. 'Now that's what I call curly!'

Alice's hair is an explosion of curls. The friends have a last look in the mirror and then they're ready to party. First the pizza arrives, thanks to Mum, who is trying very hard to hide a smile. Dad gets the film ready and then they shut the door behind them and leave the girls to their 'sleep over' party. After the film and pizza, the girls roll out their sleeping bags on the bedroom floor.

No sleeping in beds tonight! In fact, no sleeping anywhere really because the girls end up chatting throughout the night, despite Dad's repeated taps on the wall! The next morning the girls come down for breakfast yawning and bleary-eyed. Mum smiles at them and says, 'I don't know why it's called a 'sleep-over' when you try to stay awake all night! It's a good job it doesn't happen very often.' The girls have had a lovely time but they can't help but agree!

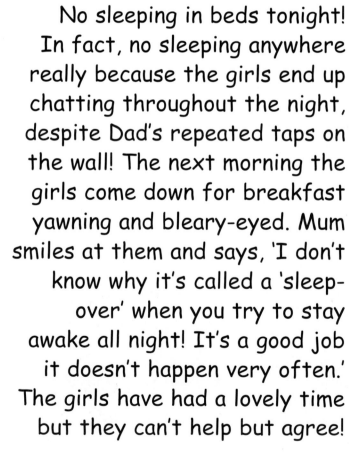

The Magic Garden

Old Mrs Perkins has an absolutely fantastic ornamental garden. There is a pretty goldfish pond that is surrounded by ceramic frogs, red and white spotted toadstools, assorted gnomes, a tiny windmill and one tall, plastic heron. Some of the gnomes stand amid the flowerbeds whilst others perch on toadstools or pose with their fishing rods around the pond. Maya and Jake can see Mrs Perkins's house from their bedroom window and have noticed something rather strange in her garden.

Each day the gnomes seem to change position. Yesterday Jake noticed the gnome with the red hat perched upon a toadstool, but today the same gnome is fishing by the windmill! And Maya is quite sure the heron by the bird table was standing in the middle of the pond yesterday! Maya and Jake have a plan to see if Mrs Perkins is moving the ornaments around at night, or if the ornaments are moving about by themselves. It's dark outside now and the children are tucked up in bed.

Mummy and Daddy think Maya and Jake are asleep but they are wide awake and waiting for the lights to go out in Mrs Perkins's house. Before bedtime the children drew a rough plan of the garden showing the positions of all the ornaments. At midnight Jake looks out of his bedroom window. The street lamps light up the garden and Jake can see that everything is in the same place. He watches for two hours before waking Maya. They take turns all night but still nothing happens.

Soon it is time to get up and the two exhausted children drag themselves out of bed. Disappointed, they eat their breakfasts and set off to school, taking one last look at Mrs Perkins's garden as they pass. Nothing has changed and Jake wonders if they just imagined everything. But as they disappear around the bend Mrs Perkins opens her front door and claps her hands three times. The ornaments burst into life, race around the garden to new positions, then change back into ornaments. Mrs Perkins chuckles and goes back into her house with her black cat!

Fairground Ballerina

The fair has come to town. Sam and Sally Swan can see the top of the helter-skelter slide just peeping over the tops of the trees. The two little swans look forward to the annual August fair and have been saving up their pocket money for weeks. Rides and stalls fill every corner of Farmer Black's field. There are red, yellow and blue flashing lights and gaily-coloured flags waving in the breeze. The rich aroma of candyfloss, toffee apples, and hotdogs is in the air.

As they pass the hoopla stall, Sally sees a beautiful ballerina doll amongst the prizes. Her jet black hair is tied up with flowers and her pretty pink tutu is studded with sequins. Sally longs to win her so she pays for twelve hooplas. She tries so hard to throw a ring over the ballerina but misses every time. Sally spends all her money and has nothing left for anything else. She trails after Sam, as he bumps his car round the dodgems, rides the painted carousel horses and slides down the enormous helter-skelter.

Sam offers his candyfloss to Sally to cheer her up, but she can only think about the doll. Before they leave the fair, Sally goes back for one last look at it. In front of the stall, half hidden in the grass, Sally sees a fat wallet. It is bulging with money. Sally sees the stallholder frantically searching for his wallet amongst the hooplas. She immediately hands the wallet over. He is so grateful that he tells Sally to choose anything she likes from his stall. Guess what she chooses? Sam and Sally have had a wonderful day.

Sammy Centipede

It is the day before the new school term begins and the jungle animals are getting their uniforms ready. The school shop has stocked up on caps, blazers, shirts and shoes - especially shoes! The queue outside the shop reaches back a long, long way because Sammy Centipede is at the front of the queue, trying on new shoes. He'll need fifty pairs of shoes! Everyone wishes they had got to the shop before Sammy. I hope there will be some shoes left for everyone else!

What is a Snowflake?

Paula the Polar Bear lives in the North Pole where snow covers everything. Paula loves the snow and wants to know more about it. Daddy Bear tells Paula that each snowflake is made of lots of tiny ice crystals and each crystal has six sides. Dad draws three shapes in the snow. Paula recognises a triangle with three sides and a square with four sides. Dad says the one with six sides is a hexagon. Paula spends hours drawing shapes in the snow until more snow falls from the sky and covers up all her patterns.

The Strange Little Horse

A herd of beautiful horses live wild in the forest. Trudging alone through the trees is a little foal who has lost his mother and wants to join the herd. The other horses make fun of the little foal because he has a strange bump in the middle of his head, and two more on his back. They don't want another mouth to feed so the foal has to leave the herd.

The foal spends the winter in the barn of a kind farmer. When spring arrives the little foal has grown tall and strong. The bump on his head is a spiral horn and the bumps on his back are a pair of magnificent wings! He's not a horse at all, he's a beautiful white unicorn. He spreads his wings and flies into the sky in search of other unicorns. As he rises above the clouds, he sees hundreds of them flying towards him.

At the front of the herd he can see his mother, she's been searching for him for months since she lost him in a blizzard. Everyone is so happy to see him. They swoop over the horses in the forest and he neighs loudly to get their attention. They wave back not recognising him, but he doesn't mind. He's just so happy because he is back where he belongs.

Maurice and the Cheese Monsters

Maurice Mouse is a scientist and his latest project is to find out if the moon is really made of cheese. He plans an expedition to test it for himself. Maurice climbs into his rocket: 10.. 9.. 8.. 7.. 6.. 5.. 4.. 3.. 2.. 1.. BLAST OFF !! Maurice shoots into space. He's on his way. He gently touches down on the moon's bright yellow surface.

Maurice takes a long deep sniff and the wonderful aroma of fresh cheese fills his nostrils. He takes out a knife and cuts a large slice out of the moon. It tastes delicious! Suddenly, shouts and screams fill the air and hoards of cheese monsters race towards him. They're angry because Maurice is eating their moon! Maurice leaps for the rocket's ladder and scrambles up the rungs as fast as he can, but the cheese monsters catch him and shake him until he falls off.

Maurice thumps to the ground with a cheese monster still gripping his leg. But when he opens his eyes he sees Mummy standing in front of him with a plate in one hand and his leg in the other! She says, 'Wake up Maurice, it's supper time!' Maurice must have been dreaming. He chuckles to himself and curls up on the sofa to enjoy a slice of cheese on toast. From the sofa, Maurice can see the moon in the night sky. It's crescent shaped. In fact, it rather looks as if someone has taken a bite out of it!

The Colourful Chameleon

It is Carly Chameleon's birthday and she has lots of presents to open. Sitting amongst the green leaves in her tree, Carly is a lovely green colour too. But as she picks up her first parcel she turns red to match the paper. When she holds the yellow ribbon, she turns yellow. The same happens for the pink, blue and purple presents. Chameleons are very clever at camouflaging themselves by colouring their skin to match their surroundings. But watch out when Carly's skin turns dark because that means she is cross and she might stick her very, very long tongue out at you!

A Different Sort of Trunk

The elephant family are moving house. Mummy tells Eddie to pack his trunk before the removal men arrive. Eddie finds a stack of boxes, packing cases, bags and suitcases in the attic. He grabs a small one and lays it on his bed. But HOW is he supposed to pack his trunk? When he closes the lid his trunk gets caught!

And WHY must he pack his trunk? It's a very useful thing to have. He can unscrew bottle tops with it, feed himself with it, carry things with it - in fact he'd be totally lost without it! Downstairs Mummy and Daddy are helping the removal men pack everything into the van. 'Have you packed that trunk yet, Eddie?' asks Mummy. She hears a muffled trumpeting noise from upstairs.

Moments later Eddie struggles downstairs with his trunk trapped in the suitcase. Mummy immediately sees Eddie's mistake and bursts out laughing. 'I meant the packing case type of trunk, you silly sausage!' she chuckles as she opens the lid and rubs Eddie's sore nose. 'Phew! That's a relief,' grins Eddie.

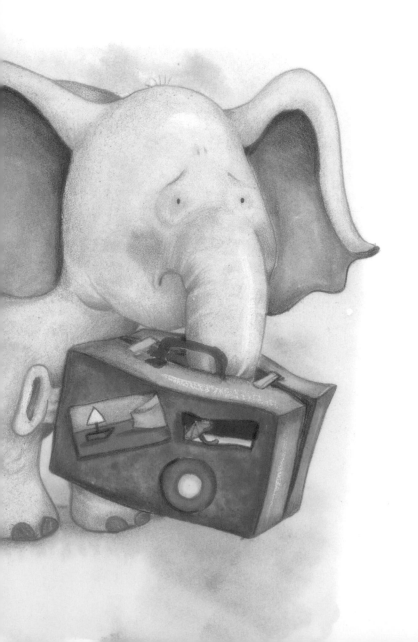

A Very Rainy Day

It has been raining all day and Jenny is really bored. She has read all her library books and done four jigsaw puzzles. She watches the rain through the window as she cuddles her dog, Bess. Two little ducks waddle down the road. They're splashing in and out of all the puddles and having a great time. Jenny sees her raincoat and boots and thinks there is no good reason why she shouldn't enjoy the rain too. She buttons up her coat, pulls on her boots and chases Bess into the garden. They play for hours and when they finally come in for tea, Jenny can't help hoping it pours down tomorrow too.

The Skeleton

Shane is digging the garden with Daddy when he unearths a small piece of bone. Daddy thinks it could part of a mouse skeleton. Shane is fascinated and wants to know more about his own bones. Daddy finds a book about the human body and flicks through it to find a diagram of the skeleton. Shane looks at the picture for ages until he has learned the names of a few of the main bones, then he draws a skeleton and labels it to show Daddy. Daddy is very impressed.

School Holidays

Stuart is a bit bored with the school holiday because most of the children in his class have gone away for the week. Stuart's family can't go on holiday because the builders are here to extend the kitchen and Daddy wants to be around to help. A big lorry dumps an enormous mound of sand on the driveway next to a pile of bricks. Stuart makes sandcastles while his daddy talks to the workmen.

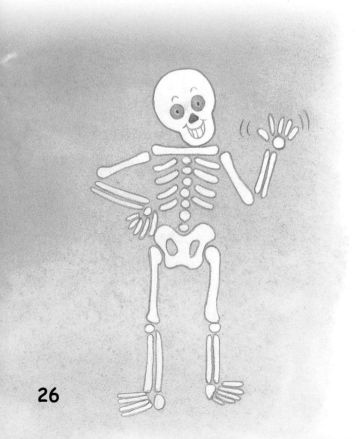

One of the builders asks Stuart to pass him a brick. Stuart has to put a yellow hard hat on before taking the brick to the man. Stuart likes helping and Daddy says it's okay, as long as he stays close to him because building sites can be dangerous. Building a wall looks hard work so Stuart goes to the kitchen and pours orange squash for the three men. Over the next few days, the extension quickly takes shape and Stuart is disappointed when the holiday ends and he has to go back to school.

At school the children take turns to tell the class what they did during the holiday. Some children had been abroad, some had visited relatives and some had gone to play schemes for the week. When it's Stuart's turn he describes the extension, the machines, the workmen and how he helped with odd jobs. Stuart thinks his holiday was by far the most fun and he even thinks he might like to be a builder when he grows up.

Farrah Frog

Farrah Frog has lots of new babies. The babies began life as frogspawn in a woodland pond, before hatching into tiny black tadpoles. The tadpoles are fat little creatures with wiggly tails, but as they get older the tails disappear and they grow arms and legs. Farrah has twenty-seven babies and she has to choose a name for each of them. She picks one name for each letter of the alphabet.

Here is a list of all the names Farrah has chosen so far:

Albert, Bella, Clarence, Daryl, Edwin, Fiona, Guy, Heather, Ian, Josie, Kevin, Lana, Michael, Nicole, Oliver, Polly, Quentin, Rachel, Scott, Tessa, Ursula, Victor, Wendy, Xavier, Yasmin, and Zach. There is one little baby left, but Farrah can't think of anymore names! She is going to let you choose the last baby's name. Write the name here

....

Farrah thinks this baby has the best name!

Moving House

Stanley and his mummy stand in the rain at the bottom of the garden and watch the removal men loading furniture into a van. It takes all morning to empty the house, then the family lock the front door and drive away to a new home. The sun starts to shine as another removal van arrives to fill the house with different furniture. The new owners spend the rest of the day dusting and cleaning.

Stanley wonders why the family wants to move. Mummy says the house became too small for the family when they had their third child. Stanley is a garden snail and carries his house on his back. As Stanley grows bigger, so does his house! Mummy and Stanley crawl down the path to a sunny spot. If it rains again they'll curl up in their shells, warm and cosy. They don't need umbrellas or new houses. Stanley is glad he's not human!

The Magical Oak

A long, long time ago there was an enchanted wood, which grew magic oak trees. These special trees could move from wood to wood, disappearing then reappearing elsewhere. If you were lucky enough to come across one of these special trees, you would see a small door at the base of the trunk, just big enough to squeeze through if you were a small child. Each door would allow you to visit Fairyland for just one hour. Best of all, you would be invisible!

When Josh and Megan's family rent a weekend holiday cottage, they find a magic oak tree at the bottom of their garden. Megan soon spots the tiny door and Josh pushes it open. Inside it's not dark at all, bright sunshine streams out of the tree! Josh pokes his head in further and sees green hills and pretty flowers. He just can't resist squeezing all the way through the door and Megan follows after him.

They decide to explore this amazing place. Fluttering down the lane are two pretty fairies and further along they come across other fairy folk going about their business. No one pays them any attention and the children soon realise they are invisible in this fairy world. They pass toadstool houses, tiny castles and elves and sprites riding colourful dragonflies and butterflies.

The lane takes them in a large circle and one hour later they find themselves back at the little door. They can hear Dad calling them in for lunch. When they tell Mum and Dad about their adventure, their parents don't believe them, so they decide to show them the tree. The tree has gone! Mum and Dad smile and go back into the cottage leaving Megan and Josh wondering if it was just a dream. Suddenly, on a puff of wind, an elf sails by on a dragonfly and disappears into the wood. The children smile: now they know it really did happen.

The Good Luck Charm

As Fairy Tinks flutters over a stream, she spies something really special on the bank. It's a four-leaf clover. She picks the leaf and pins it to her belt, knowing it should bring her good luck all day long. Above her a nasty black crow spots Tinks's pretty wings and thinks she'd be good to eat! He swoops down with an open beak and just as he's about to scoop her up, she leans forward to adjust the clover and the crow skims over her head and crashes into the water!

Tinks doesn't notice a thing as she flutters across the grass. The clover has become loose in her belt and it slips out. Tinks dives to the ground to catch it just as the bedraggled crow reaches out for her with his bony claws. He misses once again and crashes into a tree! But Tinks still hasn't noticed the horrid bird. She sees a group of children playing with fishing nets and flies over to see what they have caught. They are catching butterflies and putting them in a big jam-jar. This makes Tinks really cross.

Tinks wrestles with the lid of the jam-jar, but she's not strong enough to pull it off. Behind her the angry crow is racing up to catch her in his sharp beak. He's just about to close his beak on her when she slides off the jam-jar lid and lands on the grass. The unlucky crow rams his beak into the lid and is stuck fast. He shakes and bangs the lid until it falls to the ground. The butterflies escape and the crow decides that chasing fairies is far too dangerous.

Tinks feels sorry for the battered and bruised crow. He looks like he's had a really bad day. She offers him the four-leaf clover saying, 'I think you should have this. It's supposed to bring luck, although I can't say I've noticed anything different today!' She lays it on his knee and flies away. The grumpy crow flicks the leaf away. It catches the breeze and pokes him in the eye! I think it only works if you are nice!

Simon's First Train Journey

Daddy and Simon are going to visit Granny. She lives miles away in the city and so they have to travel by train. Simon has never been on a train before. He runs onto the platform, dragging Daddy by the hand. The railway station is packed with people and Daddy holds on tight to Simon, he doesn't want to lose him. Daddy shows Simon the ticket and points out the seat number.

Then he lets Simon find the right carriage and they climb on board. The train travels so fast that the countryside blurs into a stream of colour. They whiz through big towns and pretty villages, past ugly factories and wasteland, by farm animals and patchwork fields full of crops. All the time the train has a wonderful rhythm of its own;

Chuggity-chug, chuggity-chug, chuggity-chug.

Simon's eyelids feel heavy and he soon falls asleep. Finally the train slows down as it approaches the city station and Simon wakes up. The journey seems to have taken no time at all. Granny is waiting for them outside the ticket barrier and Simon rushes over to tell her about his journey. 'Perhaps you'll be a train driver when you're a grown-up,' Granny says with a smile. Simon can't wait!

Ice Scream

Gemma's big sister is taking her ice-skating today. Gemma has often watched her sister competing, but this is the first time she has tried it herself. The big boots seem clumsy and heavy but as soon as they touch the ice Gemma feels as if she's floating. Her sister holds her tightly as they glide around the rink and Gemma squeals with laughter. After an hour they are tired and ready to leave, but not until after one last treat. Gemma's sister buys her a big chocolate cornet. 'It's an ice scream for my very noisy little sister!' she laughs.

Percy to the Rescue

Percy Pelican lives at the seaside and hunts for fish every day. Other sea birds fish in the ocean too. Gordon Gull and his noisy friends always seem to be chasing the same fish as Percy. He doesn't like the gulls much because they are rude and make fun of his enormous bucket like beak. One afternoon, as Percy is fishing, he hears Gordon's gang screeching even louder than usual. Percy has a beak full of tasty fish and can't wait to get home for supper but he's worried that the gulls are in trouble.

He turns around and swoops down to the huddle of birds far below. Percy knows that if he lands in the water carrying so many fish it will be impossible to take off again, but when he sees Gordon nursing a broken wing he wants to help. The other gulls try to lift Gordon up, but he's too heavy. Percy drops his fish, scoops Gordon up in his beak and flies back home. Gordon is ashamed of his bad behaviour and promises to be kinder from now on. Percy thinks it is well worth losing his supper because he's made a new friend.

Lion's New Hair Do

Lion needs a haircut. His fringe is so long he can barely see through it! Sitting in the hairdressing salon, Lion flicks through the magazines and tries to pick a style. There are too many to choose from so Lion asks the other customers to decide. Crocodile thinks a curly perm would be rather nice. 'No, no,' says Cheetah. 'Short back and sides is much better!'

Snake thinks a punk hairdo would be perfect, but Elephant wants him to try a bouffant look. 'What about pigtails?' asks Boar. 'Or a pony tail?' suggests Zebra. 'I really can't decide,' Lion says to the hairdresser. 'I think I'll leave it up to you.' He squeezes his eyes tightly shut and lets the hairdresser snip away at his mane. Ten minutes later Lion opens his eyes and is delighted with the cut. The hairdresser has just tidied up his hair with a trim. Very nice Lion!

Sherlock Detective Agency

Sherlock Sheepdog is a very clever dog. The farm animals always call for him when there is a mystery to be solved. One afternoon as Sherlock dozes in the sunshine, Bertie Blackbird shakes him awake and tells him there is an emergency at the farmhouse. Sherlock leaps into action. He grabs his magnifying glass, binoculars and notebook and races into the house.

Sherlock finds Tom Cat tied to the table leg with a sticky note stuck to his forehead. It reads,

'LEAVE FIVE KILOS OF BEST CHEESE BY THE STABLE DOOR OR KITTY CAT GETS IT!!!'

Sherlock unties Tom and asks if he recognised any of the kidnappers. Tom shakes his head because it was dark and they all wore masks. Sherlock scans the floor with his magnifying glass. He sees faint paw prints and a few hairs from Kitty.

Sherlock follows the trail across the wooden floor and down the stone steps into the farmyard. He examines the stables through the binoculars and sees some movement in the rafters. Sherlock creeps over to the stable door and quietly climbs the ladder to the loft. In a dark corner, he sees four pairs of eyes frowning at him. Sherlock takes a deep breath and barks as loudly as he can.

Four huge rats squeal as they escape through windows and doors, leaving a very cross Kitty Cat tied up in the straw. Kitty is very pleased to be rescued and shows Sherlock the rats' hoard of stolen goods. There are buns and biscuits, carrots and cakes and pastries and pies. The Farmer is so pleased to be rid of the rats that he lets Sherlock have all the food. Sherlock throws a party for everyone and the animals insist he has the biggest slice of cake.

39

Little Angel

Angela is a happy little angel. She lives in Heaven with angels from every country in the world. It's a wonderful place, full of kindness and love, where everyone is content, nothing bad ever happens and the sun always shines. Like all angels, Angela hears prayers from people on earth and wants to do her best to cheer them up.

So, when Angela hears a prayer she blows a kiss and sends it high into the night sky, where it turns into a shooting star. If you look out of your window tonight, you might be lucky enough to see one racing through the sky. The people who see Angela's shooting star always feel much more cheerful afterwards. No matter what has happened, it's bound to make you smile!

Bruno Bear

Bruno Bear collects musical instruments even though he cannot play any of them. He just enjoys hanging them on the walls of his cave. Bruno's cave is quite small and because the instruments take up so much room, Bruno is worried he may have to get rid of a few. Esther Elephant is coming to tea this afternoon, she's rather large and Bruno is not sure she will fit into his crowded cave.

At 3 o'clock Esther arrives and squeezes herself into a chair, knocking Bruno's instruments off the wall and flattening them underfoot! She settles down to Bruno's cream buns and coconut milk and after a lovely tea waves goodbye to him. Bruno tidies up his flattened instruments with a big smile on his face. He hangs them all up again and they take up much less space, he now has room for lots more!

Lost At Sea

Jason and Martha take an inflatable dinghy to the beach. Mum and Dad let them play in it as long as they stay at the edge of the shore and don't float out to sea. The breaking waves toss the little dinghy up and down and the children pretend they are pirates sailing a stormy ocean. They don't notice the tide gently pulling them out to sea. Martha sees how far they have drifted and starts to panic.

Jason hugs Martha, but he worries too when he sees a large triangular fin steadily approaching the dinghy. Jason has read about sharks and can imagine row upon row of sharp white teeth. The fin sinks below the water and seconds later a large grey head with a friendly smile pops up beside them. It's a dolphin! Jason has read about dolphins too. They are intelligent creatures that are renowned for helping sailors lost at sea.

The dolphin nudges the dinghy toward the shore with its beak. They bump onto the sand and the dolphin splashes back out to sea. Dad is engrossed in a newspaper and Mum is sunbathing with her eyes closed. No one noticed they were gone! As they drag the dinghy back up the beach, the children decide never to use the dinghy unless Mum or Dad are keeping a very close eye on them.

Best Of Friends

Rex enjoys life. He takes his human, Bert, into the garden and basks in the sunshine while Bert digs happily amongst the flowers. At five o'clock it will be time to take Bert for a walk. Bert is quite old now but Rex gives him three good walks each day. Rex has spent a lot of time training his human. Bert walks well on the lead and knows how to throw balls and sticks. Rex is very fond of Bert. They have been together for a long time. He knows that man is a dog's best friend. He gives Bert a friendly pat then they both close their eyes and doze in the afternoon sunshine.

Salt and Pepper

Salt and Pepper are two little mice who live next door to each other in Daisy Wood. Salt is a very kind mouse but Pepper is a very selfish mouse. One chilly October morning the two mice are playing together in the wood when old Mrs Badger pokes her head out of her doorway and asks the mice to nip down to the farm to collect some fresh milk and eggs for her. Pepper says the farm is too far away and refuses to go, but kind hearted Salt sets off immediately. It will take hours to get there, so Mrs Badger gives him a sandwich and a bottle of water to take along.

By lunchtime, Salt is very hungry and sits on a stone at the side of the track to eat his sandwich. He notices a tired old rabbit slowly making her way up the track towards him. The old rabbit gazes longingly at the food as she shuffles past. Salt feels sorry for her and offers to share the food. The old rabbit is delighted and sits down next to Salt. Once they have eaten, the old rabbit leaps to her feet and throws off her furry coat, revealing herself to be a little fairy. The fairy waves her magic wand and a large wheelbarrow appears, piled high with food. The food is for Salt for being so kind. Salt thanks the fairy and runs back home, pushing the wheelbarrow.

44

Salt shares the food with all the woodland creatures. Pepper is very jealous of Salt's good fortune and so the very next day he sets off down the same track. After a while he sees a duck sitting on the path with an injured foot. As he walks past, the duck asks if he will help her to get back to her pond. The detour will take Pepper well away from the road and Pepper wants to find the old rabbit that turns into a fairy, so he refuses to help and goes on his way. As he starts to leave, the duck jumps to her feet and shakes off her feathers to reveal a cross little fairy. The fairy waves her wand and a wheelbarrow full of wonderful food appears.

Pepper is delighted and races back home without even saying thank you. As Pepper gets closer to home he notices the food beginning to rot. By the time he reaches his front door the food smells dreadful and all the neighbours hold their noses and tell him to throw it away. As Pepper gets rid of the food he realises what a selfish mouse he's been. He decides to be kinder from now on. The fairy watches Pepper and thinks that he's learned his lesson. She leaves a tasty red apple on his doorstep and flies away. When Pepper sees it on his step he cuts it in two and shares it with Salt because that's what friends do!

The Big Party

Marvin Monzta has a rather unusual home, his family live in a tumbledown castle that sits on top of a wooded hill, high above the village. Tonight, Marvin is throwing a party for all his school friends. Although the guests are nervous about visiting the spooky castle, they all want to go to the party because Marvin is such a fun friend to have. He's very different from all the other children in the village.

Most people have pet dogs and cats but Marvin has pet worms and bats! Most people travel by bus or car but Marvin usually arrives in a dusty, black coach pulled by wild black stallions! Most people wear anoraks or jackets but Marvin wears a long black cloak with a rich red lining! And most people like feeding the ducks in the park but Marvin likes feeding the bats in the dark!

46

At seven o'clock, the guests knock on the heavy wooden doors and wait as bats and owls circle overhead. A solemn butler, holding a flickering candle, creaks open the door and points them in the direction of the ballroom. The corridors are draped in cobwebs and mice scuttle across the dusty floorboards. Portraits of bygone ancestors glower down at them from ancient frames as they tiptoe past, huddled together and wide-eyed with anticipation. The ballroom doors slowly open as the children approach.

Coffins and gravestones lean against the walls. Skeletons and broomsticks hang from the ceiling amongst dusty cobwebs. A giant cauldron occupies the centre of the room and in front of it stands a black cat and Marvin holding a big book of spells. The children seem dumbstruck. Suddenly Marvin yells, 'HAPPY HALLOWEEN EVERYONE!' and the fancy dress party begins!

Pixie in a Pocket

Pixie is Sean's pet gerbil. He's rather like a big mouse with huge back legs. Sean plays with Pixie in his bedroom for half an hour each day before breakfast. Pixie is being naughty today and won't go back into his cage. Sean looks all around his bedroom but can't find Pixie, not even in the bookcase where he likes chewing books. He's hiding in Sean's jacket pocket. After breakfast, Sean pulls his jacket on and heads off to Tim's house.

Pixie peeps over the edge of Sean's pocket and the sun warms his face as he watches the birds and butterflies in the sky and the fast cars on the road. He really enjoys the journey until they arrive at Tim's house. Tim owns four cats! As soon as they smell Pixie they jump up at Sean. Sean wonders what they want and digs around his pocket, pulling out a terrified little gerbil. Pixie wants to be back in his cosy little cage so Sean tucks him up safely and runs back home with him. Silly Pixie!

Silly Nita

Nita lives in the snowy Arctic. She shares her igloo home with her mum, dad and baby brother. Furs, blankets and a small fire keep the igloo nice and warm, but Nita thinks a bigger fire would be much cosier. One day, before they all leave on a hunting trip, Nita secretly builds up the fire. She thinks it will be lovely and warm when they return.

Nita's fire is a bit too warm for the icy igloo and the walls soon start to melt. When the family return, the igloo has gone and all that is left is a big puddle of water. Nita is very sorry and wants to help build another igloo. It takes hours to carve out more big blocks of ice, but Nita works twice as hard as Mum and Dad to make up for her silly mistake. By bedtime the igloo is ready and everyone crawls under their furs and blankets and has a VERY long sleep.

The Forgetful Ladybird

Larry and Libby Ladybird are having a race. The first to reach Aunty Linda's house wins. Libby takes one path and Larry takes another. Libby is very forgetful and can never remember the fastest way to get to Aunty Linda's. She climbs Molehill Mountain, skirts around the pit in the middle and slides down the other side into dense forest. Keeping one eye on the sun to guide her, she soon reaches the steep sides of a large, water-filled crater and scrambles to the top.

Dog Bowl Lake is quite close to Aunty Linda's home and Libby thinks she'll make it before nightfall. A stray leaf makes a perfect boat to cross the lake and at the other side she slides down Spade Handle Hill and races the last few steps to number three Geranium Row. Aunty Linda is waiting with a mug of hot chocolate and to her surprise, so is Larry! 'How did you get here so quickly?' she asks. 'I flew,' says Larry. 'Silly me,' says Libby. 'I forgot I have wings!' What a forgetful ladybird she is!

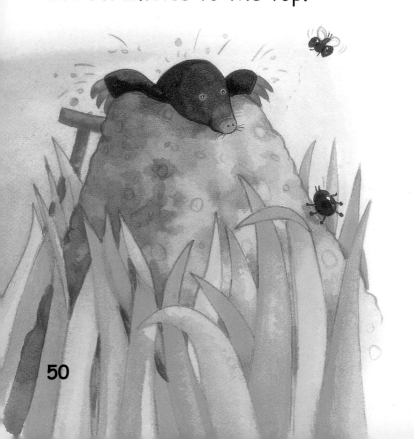

Little Dizzy

Hattie Hadrosaur sits on her nest waiting for six large, leathery eggs to hatch. Over the next two days five baby hadrosaurs emerge, but one egg remains intact. Hattie is very busy looking after her new babies and finds it harder and harder to sit on the last egg.

One morning whilst Hattie is playing with her babies, a greedy pteranodon swoops down and steals the egg. The egg is heavy and the pteranodon can't fly very far with it. Eventually the egg slips out of her claws and tumbles through the air to land in the branches of a fir tree. Down below, a triceratops trundles over to the tree and scratches his back on the rough bark.

The tree shakes violently and the egg wobbles free and bounces into the long grass. A herd of long necked brontosaurs see the egg rolling towards them and play football with it. They kick the egg around the cliff top until the smallest brontosaurus accidentally kicks it over the cliff edge. The egg crashes down the slope and splashes into a fast flowing river.

A plesiosaur swims to the egg and flicks it out of the water with her strong tail. The bruised and battered egg flies through the air to land with a satisfying 'plop', back in Hattie's nest, just as she returns with her babies. Then the egg starts to move all by itself. Suddenly the shell breaks and a tiny, wobbly baby struggles out. The baby is none the worse for his adventure, but he does look a little dizzy. And that's what Hattie decides to call him - Little Dizzy!

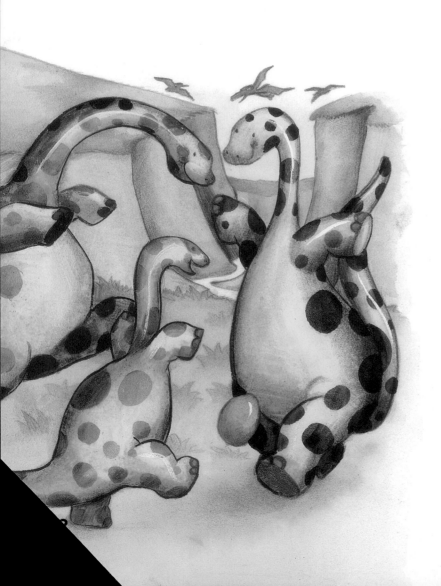

The Old Lighthouse

Lenny Lighthouse was once a very handsome and important building. He was built over two hundred years ago, on an outcrop of rock by the sea, alongside a busy shipping lane. His job was to warn ships of the dangerous rocks hiding beneath the water. But as the years went by ships sailed different routes and Lenny was no longer needed.

Today Lenny is just a worn out shell. His paint is peeling and all his windows are broken. He hasn't seen anyone for ages. But this morning Lenny's rock is buzzing with workmen and traffic. He is given a new coat of paint; the lamp, windows and doors are replaced and a large sign is screwed into his wall. It says this is a site of historical interest. Fantastic! Lenny will have lots of visitors and never be lonely again.

A New Baby Sister

My mummy has a new baby and Daddy and I are going to the hospital to see her. I have made a card with a big red heart on it for Mummy and I'm giving my very best dolly to my new little sister. Daddy is taking Mummy's favourite flowers. Look! There's Mummy, in the bed by the big window. She's cuddling the baby. I didn't know she would be this tiny. She's even smaller than my best dolly!

I sit on the bed next to Mummy and she shows me how to hold the baby. She has a wrinkled, little face and blue eyes and fingers and toes which are soooo small and soooo cute. I say to Mummy and Daddy, 'We should call her Tina, because she is so tiny.' Mummy and Daddy like the name very much, so Tina is her name and I think she's the best little sister in the world!

Night Monsters

Jasmine snores gently. She and Teddy are cosily tucked up in a nice warm bed, on this chilly night. An owl hoots as it flies past her window and the noise wakes her up with a start. Jasmine's night lamp has been turned off and the only light in the room comes from the pale moon shining through half closed curtains. The once familiar bedroom now seems full of unfriendly objects. Jasmine stares in horror at a monstrous shape, which has appeared at the foot of her bed.

Jasmine clutches Teddy and cowers behind the duvet as the monster fades into the shadows, leaving wide staring eyes. In a moment of bravery Jasmine reaches out and punches the switch on the night lamp. Light floods the room and Jasmine finds herself face to face with ....THE MIRROR!!!

The wide staring eyes were hers! She scribbles a note and props it against her night lamp. It reads:

PLEASE NEVER, EVER TURN MY NIGHT LIGHT OFF, (OR AT LEAST NOT UNTIL I'M SIX). LOVE JASMINE XXX

Greedy Ghost

Peter's granny lives in a house that is over two hundred years old. It's a house with a lot of history and Peter loves exploring the old-fashioned rooms with dark, dusty cellars and the cluttered, cobwebbed attic. Peter's two brothers tease him with scary ghost stories, but they don't worry Peter. Today he has a mystery to solve. A tub of strawberry ice cream vanished from Granny's fridge yesterday morning, a packet of biscuits went missing last night and a huge slice of chocolate cake disappeared from the pantry this morning!

Peter makes a list of the missing items and goes down for breakfast. Granny leaves two slices of buttered toast on Peter's plate while he is pouring a glass of milk. But when Peter sits at the table there is only half a slice of toast left! What's going on? Peter decides to set a trap. He secretly makes a tasty looking sandwich, thickly spread with mustard and extra hot chilli peppers. He leaves the sandwich on the kitchen table and turns away to wash the dishes.

When he looks back, the plate is empty! Peter's brothers are kicking a ball about in the garden, so they haven't eaten it. Granny is quietly reading the paper and sipping a cup of tea, so she hasn't eaten it. Peter is puzzled. He runs upstairs to clean his teeth and hears someone coughing and spluttering in the bathroom. He pulls open the door, catching the food thief still holding half of the sandwich.

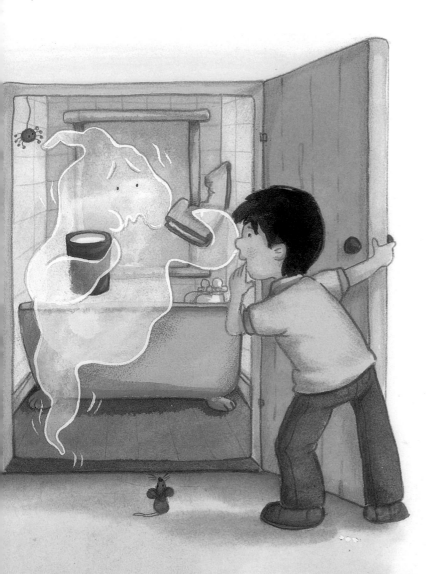

Peter can't believe his eyes. The thief is a ghost! The ghost quickly hides the sandwich behind his back, but ghosts are transparent so that doesn't work! The ghost is embarrassed and apologises. Peter doesn't mind at all, he's just fascinated to see a real ghost. This house has lots of secrets but Peter's secret is the best. He keeps his ghostly friend supplied with sandwiches and in return the ghost tells Peter all the secrets he knows about the house.

Garden Bath Time

'You all need a good bath!' says Mummy, as Mishka, the German Shepherd dog, pads across the kitchen floor, followed by two grubby children and three sets of footprints. But the children grumble so much about having a bath that Mummy thinks of a clever way to clean them up. She fills a bucket full of water and asks Jack and Gemma to wash the dog outside in the garden. Mishka soon disappears under a blanket of foam.

Mishka stands patiently while the children take turns rinsing off the bubbles with a hosepipe. A beautifully clean dog now stands next to two grubby children, but Mummy isn't too worried as she knows what will happen next. Mishka gives herself an enormous shake. It starts at her head and works its way down to her tail. Water flies off in all directions and the children are completely soaked - and clean! Mission accomplished, thinks Mummy as she hands out dry towels!

Wait and See

One morning Parrot flies to Lion's den and asks if she could have a clawful of strong hairs from his mane.
'Of course you can,' says Lion. 'What do you want them for?'
'Wait and see,' says Parrot.
Then Parrot flies into Bear's cave and asks him if she could have a clawful of straw and dried leaves from the floor of his cave.
'Of course you can,' says Bear. 'What do you want them for?'
'Wait and see,' says Parrot.

Next, Parrot flies to Flamingo's pond and asks if she could have some soft pink feathers.
'Of course you can,' says Flamingo. 'But what do you want them for?'
'Wait and see,' says Parrot. The next day Parrot invites Lion, Bear and Flamingo for tea. When the three friends arrive at Parrot's tree they see why she asked for all those things. Parrot has made a beautiful new nest, which is strong, warm and just right for her two newborn chicks. 'Now you know what I wanted everything for!' laughs Parrot.

Stone Age Adventure

Maku is seven years old. His family share a cave with four other families. Maku is the youngest of three brothers and longs to be old enough to join his father and the older boys on hunting trips. Instead he has to stay at home with his mother and sister, gathering wood for the communal fire. He watches enviously as the hunting party leaves, scrambling down the hillside armed with long spears.

The women crowd around the fire so no-one notices as Maku quietly slips away. He follows the men at a safe distance as they cross the valley floor, tracking a herd of hairy mammoths. These gigantic beasts with their enormous curving tusks are the ancestors of modern day elephants. One mammoth will provide enough meat to feed the families for many weeks and its fur will keep them warm throughout the long harsh winter.

From behind a tree, Maku watches as the men separate a mammoth from its herd and close in. But Maku is not the only observer. Across the valley a sinister beast slowly creeps towards the men. It's a sabre-toothed tiger, man's greatest enemy! Long, sharp fangs hang down either side of its mouth and fearsome claws arm each paw. No-one but Maku has seen the danger!

Maku storms down the hillside shrieking and clattering over stones, making as much noise as possible. The mammoth breaks through the circle of startled men and escapes. Maku's father is about to yell at him when someone spots the tiger. The men attack, throwing their spears and scaring it away. Maku is swept up into his father's arms. He has saved the day. His father is so pleased that he decides to let Maku come along on the next hunt as a lookout. Maku is very proud and vows to be the best lookout ever.

Sally's Secret Passage

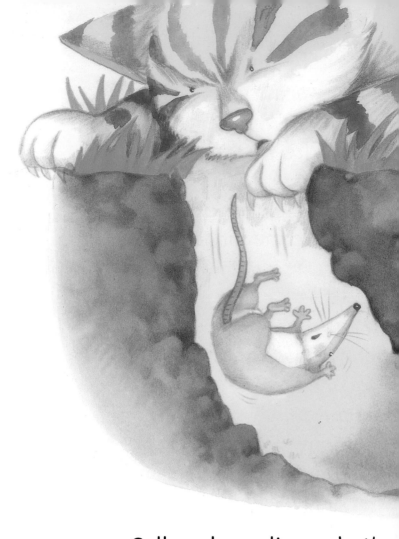

Sally Shrew scurries through the wood, leaping over gnarled tree roots and crispy, dried leaves, which swirl around in gusts of chilly December wind. She must reach Aunt Shirley's nest before night-time because it's too dangerous to travel in the dark when owls and foxes like to hunt. Sally is in such a hurry that she doesn't see the big ginger cat quietly stalking her.

Sally only realises what's happening when a dark shadow falls over her. Suddenly the cat pounces and Sally veers to her left to avoid being caught in the sharp claws. The chase is on and the cat is much faster than Sally. But Sally swerves left and right, dodging low branches which slow the cat down. She rounds an oak tree, stumbles over loose pebbles and finds herself tumbling down a deep hole in the ground.

Sally rolls head over heels into a warm furry body in a nest of straw. Sally has fallen into Rocky Rabbit's burrow. Rocky dusts Sally down and glares up the tunnel at the ginger cat. Luckily, the cat is far too big to squeeze down the tunnel, but his paws claw dangerously at the entrance as he tries to reach them. Sally's safe here but she worries that there isn't a way out!

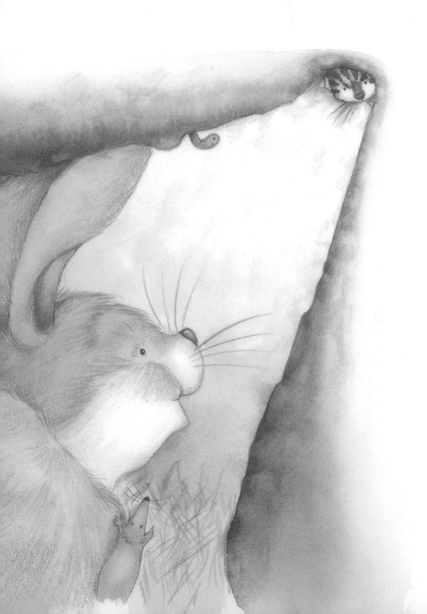

Rocky isn't at all bothered. Whilst the cat spits and claws at the entrance, Rocky digs another passage in the opposite direction. It's a very long passage and when Rocky finally comes up to the surface, Sally sees she is right next to Aunt Shirley's nest. Fantastic! Rocky is happy for Sally to use his burrow whenever she likes. And that big ginger cat never did work out how Sally disappeared. I bet he's still prowling outside Rocky's burrow now!

Mumbo Jumbo's Mixed Up Spells

Like most dragons, Mumbo Jumbo can do magic. Unlike most dragons, Mumbo gets dreadfully muddled up when he recites a spell, and they always go wrong. The fairy folk rely on dragons to help them out with their special spells so dragons are usually kept busy. Except for Mumbo. No one asks him for help after his last two disastrous spells.

Last week, a pixie asked for a spell for a new hat and Mumbo had given him a blue cat! And yesterday when a fairy asked for a gold wand she ended up standing in a cold pond! Mumbo is close to tears when Mummy Dragon gives him a small blue box, which she hopes will cheer him up. Inside the box is a pair of spectacles. When Mumbo puts them on he can read the spell book perfectly. No more mistakes! Now Mumbo Jumbo is the busiest dragon in the village.